OLLIE & MOON

DIANE KREDENSOR

with photographs by SANDRA KRESS

Tee-hee!

Random House New York

llie and Moon are best friends.
Moon loves surprises, and Ollie loves to surprise Moon.
One time he surprised her with a spaghetti cake—for no reason.

Another time he surprised her with
a performance of Irish folk dance.

Ollie even surprised Moon when
he wasn't trying to surprise her.

As much as Moon loves getting surprises,
she loves trying to guess what they are even more.

Once she even found her birthday present—
two days before her birthday.
Ollie had hidden it under Stanley.

bzzz
bzzz

One day Ollie buzzed Moon's intercom. "I have a surprise for you!" he told her.

"Oh, goody, goody, goody, goody!" said Moon. "I'll be right out."

While Ollie waited on the sidewalk, Moon carefully picked out a hat to wear—the silly one.

"Ollie, guess which hat I'm wearing!" Moon said through the intercom.

Ollie peeked in Moon's
window. "The silly one," he said.
Ollie wasn't much for guessing.

"So, where's my surprise?" Moon asked, stepping outside.

She looked all around.

She looked over Ollie and under Ollie, but she didn't see a surprise.

"I have to take you to it," said Ollie.

"Let's go!"

GRRRRRRR

Ollie's stomach was growling, so they stopped at
the *fromagerie* to buy some Brie.

"Is my surprise *cheese*?" Moon guessed.

"Nope. But your surprise *is* round," Ollie replied.

"Aha!" Moon proclaimed. "My surprise is . . .
ROUND."

"Yes, but that's not all it is," Ollie said as they
continued down the street.

On the Métro, Ollie tapped his toe to some funky music.
Whenever Ollie heard music, he couldn't help but dance.
He even tried out a few new moves.

"Hey," said Moon. "Is my surprise musical?"

"As a matter of fact, it *is*," said Ollie.

"Aha!" Moon cried. "So my surprise is . . .
ROUND *and* MUSICAL."

"You're right, but that's not all it is," Ollie said,
and they hit the streets again.

They passed Stanley by the fruit stand. He was buying apples and bananas.

"Hello, Stanley," said Ollie.

"Bonjour," replied Stanley.

"Hey," said Moon. "Is my surprise red or yellow?"

"As a matter of fact, it has lots of colors," said Ollie.

"Aha!" Moon cried. "So my surprise is . . .
ROUND and MUSICAL
and it has LOTS OF COLORS."
"True! But that's not all," Ollie said as they
continued on their way.

Walking through a park, they came upon some chess players.

"Hey," said Moon. "Does my surprise have fur, hooves, or feathers?"

"As a matter of fact, it has all three," said Ollie.

"Aha!" Moon cried. "So my surprise is . . .
ROUND and MUSICAL,
it has LOTS OF COLORS, *and* it has
FUR, HOOVES, and FEATHERS!"

"Yup, but that's not all," Ollie said
as they went on their merry way.

I'm getting tired
of guessing!

Ollie knew just the thing to
cheer up Moon. Snapshots!

"Hey," said Moon. "Is my surprise bright with lights?"

"As a matter of fact, it's very bright," said Ollie.

"Aha!" Moon cried. "So my surprise is . . .
ROUND and MUSICAL,
it has LOTS OF COLORS,
it has FUR, HOOVES, and FEATHERS,
and it's BRIGHT with LIGHTS!"

Yes, but that's not all it—

Ollie slipped and dropped his Brie.

The Brie
rolled round
and round,
down the stairs.

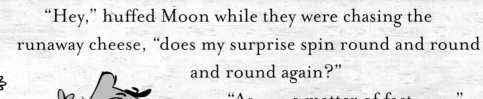

"Hey," huffed Moon while they were chasing the
runaway cheese, "does my surprise spin round and round
and round again?"

"As . . . a matter of fact . . . ,"
Ollie puffed, "it . . . does!"

"Aha!" Moon cried. "So my surprise is . . .
ROUND and MUSICAL,
it has LOTS OF COLORS,
it has FUR, HOOVES, and FEATHERS,
it's BRIGHT with LIGHTS,
and it SPINS round and round
and round again!"

"Ollie, I can read you like a book,"
said Moon. "I know what my surprise is—
it's an elephant on a unicycle juggling animals
while playing the French horn!"

"Nope," replied Ollie. "Good guess, though."

"Whew!" said Moon. "I don't really have space for an elephant in my apartment."

"Almost there . . . ," said Ollie.

Just then, they turned the corner, and there before Moon's eyes was the best surprise ever. . . .

A CAROUSEL!

"Ta-da!" crowed Ollie. "Happy surprise, Moon!"

SMAK!

Moon loved her carousel ride—even more than she loved guessing.

And Ollie was so very happy that Moon hadn't guessed what it was— otherwise it wouldn't have been a surprise.

THE END

H.K., this one's for you.
And a special thanks to
Emma and Dadoo.
—D.K.